2011

Hoedown Showdown

by Kelli Chipponeri
illustrated by Vince DePorter and Barry Goldberg

Ready-to-Read

Simon Spotlight/Nickelodeon
New York   London   Toronto   Sydney

visit us at www.abdopublishing.com

Reinforced library bound edition published in 2008 by Spotlight, a division of ABDO Publishing Group, 8000 West 78th Street, Edina, Minnesota 55439. Published by agreement with Simon Spotlight, an imprint of Simon & Schuster Children's Publishing Division.

SIMON SPOTLIGHT

An imprint of Simon & Schuster Children's Publishing Division
1230 Avenue of the Americas, New York, NY 10020

Library of Congress Cataloging-in-Publication Data
This title was previously cataloged with the following information:
Chipponeri, Kelli.
  Hoedown showdown / by Kelli Chipponeri.
    p. cm. -- (Ready-to-read. Level 2; #8)
  "Based on the TV series SpongeBob SquarePants created by Steven Hillenburg as seen on Nickelodeon."
  I. SpongeBob SquarePants (Television program). II. Title. III. Series.
PZ7.C44513 Hoe 2006
[Fic]--dc22   2005002685

ISBN-13: 978-1-59961-444-1 (reinforced library bound edition)
ISBN-10: 1-59961-444-8 (reinforced library bound edition)

All Spotlight books have reinforced library binding
and are manufactured in the United States of America.

SpongeBob and Patrick were excited.
The Bikini Bottom Rodeo was tonight!

"I am excited to be in the
sea horse rodeo," said SpongeBob.

"I can't wait to ride the giant clam!" Patrick said.

"Are you ready to do the square-dance calls for the hoedown?" asked Patrick.

"Of course," replied SpongeBob.
But he really wasn't—he had
forgotten that he was the caller!
"Uh, Patrick, maybe we should
get ready," said SpongeBob.

After they got dressed, SpongeBob and Patrick were all set to go.

SpongeBob and Patrick arrived
at the rodeo. First they went to
the sea horse corral. SpongeBob
showed off his skills on the sea horse
and came in third place!

Then they stopped by the
giant clam.
At first Patrick held on tight.

But then he let go to fix his hat—
and fell off the clam!

Finally they went to
the square-dance tent
for the hoedown.
"Hi, boys!" called Sandy Cheeks.
"SpongeBob, are you ready to be
the square-dance caller?"

"Ready? Uh, yes, I'm ready!"
said SpongeBob.
"I can hardly wait,"
said Squidward.

SpongeBob went up to the mike.
"Uh, ahem. Well, I guess I should
get started," he said.
"Please find a partner."

The Bikini Bottom Uptown
Hoedown Band began to play.
SpongeBob looked at the dancers.
Everyone looked back at him.
SpongeBob cleared his throat.
He didn't know what to say next.

Then he remembered something
he had seen on TV a long time ago.
"Swing your partner to and fro,"
SpongeBob called. "Step to the right
and away we go!"

To his surprise, the dancers did what he said! They held hands and skipped in a circle until they came back to where they had started.

"Now do what?" SpongeBob wondered out loud.

The dancers thought he called, "Now doughnut!"

Not sure what to do,
they all skipped over to
the snack table.
The dancers crashed into one another
as they reached for the doughnuts.

"No, come back!" yelled SpongeBob.
But the dancers heard, "Now,
kick back!"
The dancers looked at one another
and kicked their legs backward.
"Hey, watch out," yelled Squidward
as Patrick kicked him.

Mr. Krabs lost his balance.
Sandy tried to help but
got pinched by Mr. Krabs's claws.
"Ouch!" cried Sandy.

"Stop! Stop!" SpongeBob yelled.

But the dancers heard, "Chop-chop!"

They started chopping at one another.

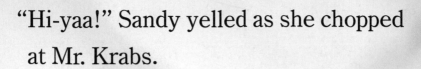

"Hi-yaa!" Sandy yelled as she chopped
  at Mr. Krabs.
"Ow!" yelped Mr. Krabs.

SpongeBob was about to give up.
Everyone was fighting instead of
dancing!

Then SpongeBob had an idea.
He grabbed a doughnut
and walked over to the dancers.
"Stop, everyone!" he called out.
He took a deep breath.
"Just follow me," he said.

"Here's the doughnut.

"This is how you kick back.

"And here's how you chop-chop!"

"Now, are you ready?" asked SpongeBob.

"Ready!" replied the dancers.

SpongeBob started calling,
"Swing your partner to and fro.
Step to the right and away we go!"

"Now, doughnut!" he called.
The group held hands and
began shuffling in a circle
to the right.

SpongeBob was happy.
He was calling a square dance!

"That was pretty fancy calling!"
   said Sandy.
"You could say I learned on my feet,"
   SpongeBob said.
"So let's do another dance—
   with new moves!" said Sandy.